Queen of the Fog

A Central City Saga

C.M. PEREIDA

QUEEN OF THE FOG - A CENTRAL CITY SAGA

Published by Central City Project Management

STAFFORDSHIRE

Central City - *Queen of The Fog*

Chapter I The Big Game

WOLF 26 NEWS — LIVE PROMO SEGMENT

The camera light blinked red. Caroline MacGyver straightened her blazer, smoothed her hair, and flashed the kind of smile that made Central City trust her weather reports even when she was wrong.

“Good evening, Central City!” she chirped, voice bright enough to cut through the thick winter fog rolling across Staffordshire Stadium. “I'm Caroline MacGyver with Wolf 26 News and Central City News Talk Radio — and we are broadcasting live at the biggest post-season tradition in the Valley: the annual showdown between Central City College and Central California State University!”

Behind her, the stadium lights glowed like a halo in the mist, and the crowd noise was already building into a low, excited rumble.

“This year, the Central City Staffies will host the Mastiffs right here at Staffordshire Stadium,” she continued. “And trust me, folks, the energy is electric. The rivalry is real, the stakes are high, and the food truck plaza is already packed. If you're hungry, this is the place to be — everything from

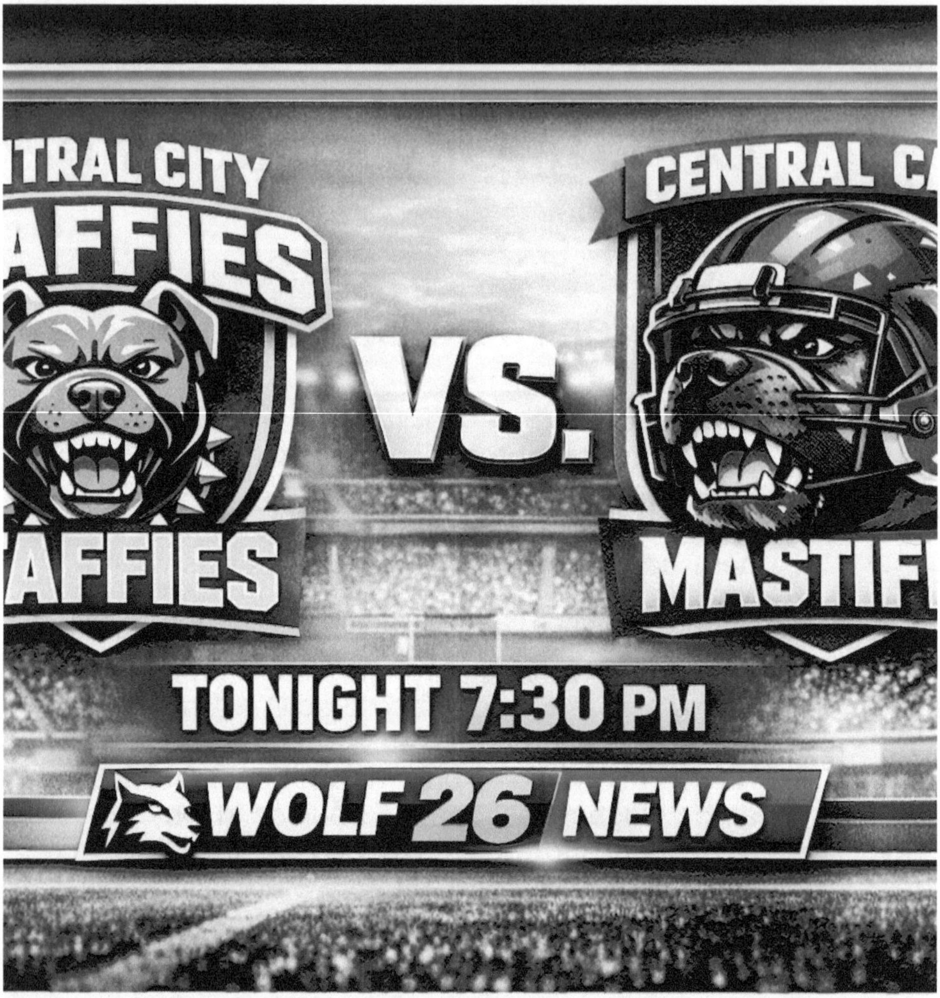

TRAL CITY
AFFIES
AFFIES
VS.
CENTRAL C
MASTIFF
TONIGHT 7:30 PM
WOLF 26 NEWS

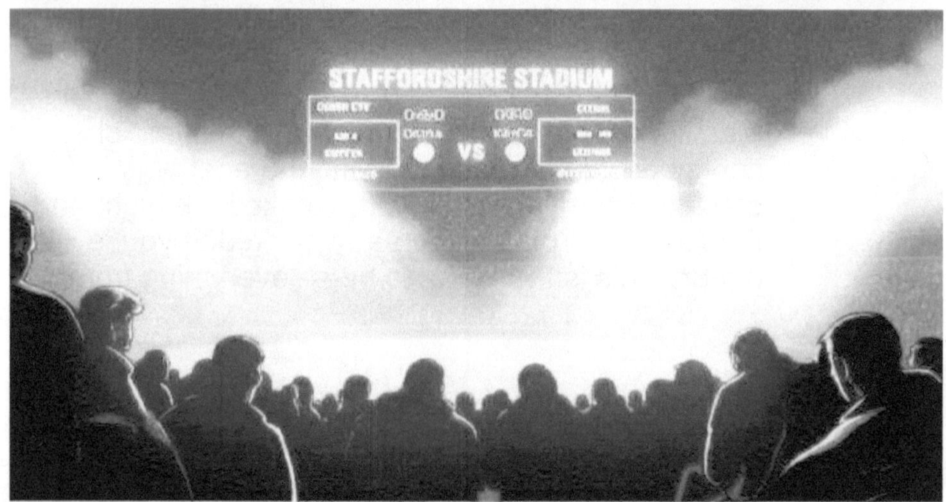

tri-tip nachos to Molten Lava Tacos to the famous Bulldog Burrito."

She shifted her stance, letting the camera catch the stadium entrance behind her.

"Now, keep your eyes on a few rising stars tonight.

CCSU's quarterback, Tyler 'Northside' Navarro, is drawing major attention — a senior from Redwood Bay High, one of Central City's biggest rivals. Scouts say he's got an arm like a cannon and legs like a sprinter. And on the Staffies' side, freshman running back Jacob Ortiz is expected to make waves after a breakout season."

She paused, letting the crowd roar punctuate her words.

"It's the weekend after the Super Bowl, but here in Central City, this is the big game. Stay tuned — kickoff is in just under an hour. Reporting live, I'm Caroline MacGyver. Back to you in the studio."

The camera light clicked off.

Caroline exhaled, shoulders dropping. "And that," she muttered, "is how you sell a football game."

Something in the Fog

She packed up her mic, slung her bag over her shoulder, and headed toward the glowing row of food trucks. The fog was thicker here, clinging to the asphalt and curling around her ankles like something alive.

She spotted him immediately — her uncle, Eddie Vega. He stood near the churro truck with his hands in his jacket pockets and his baseball cap pulled low. He looked like a man trying not to be recognized, which was funny considering half the city listened to his late-night radio show, *The Vega Frequency*, where he talked about ghosts, cryptids, and the supernatural history of the Valley.

He waved when he saw her. “Leeney!”

She blinked. “You actually came.”

“Of course I came,” he said, pulling her into a hug.

“You’re my favorite niece.”

“I’m your only niece.”

“Exactly.”

She stepped back, studying him. He looked tired — more than usual. And Eddie Vega was always tired, the kind of tired that came from staying up until three in the morning talking about shadow people and haunted orchards.

“You doing okay?” she asked.

He shrugged. “I’m here on business. And personal. Mostly business.”

She raised an eyebrow. “Business? At a football game?”

He leaned in, lowering his voice. “The fog.”

Caroline groaned. “Oh no.”

“Oh yes,” he said, eyes gleaming. “This isn’t normal fog. It’s thicker. Heavier. It’s moving wrong.”

“Fog doesn’t move wrong.”

CHURRO

"This fog does." She crossed her arms. "Uncle Eddie…" "My grandfather told me stories," he said, ignoring her tone. "About the old days. Before Central City was Central City. When the Vampire Nation ruled these lands. They used the fog as cover, as camouflage, as a hunting ground."

Caroline stared at him.

He stared back, deadly serious.

Then she snorted. "You are so dramatic."

He grinned. "Runs in the family."

She rolled her eyes, but affection softened the gesture. She loved him for this — for the wild theories, the late-night calls, the way he believed in things most people laughed at. She believed too, though she'd never admit it out loud. Not yet.

"Come on," she said. "Let's get food before you start telling me the fog is whispering your name."

Eddie didn't laugh.

He looked past her, toward the stadium and the fog. For a moment — just a moment — Caroline thought she saw something shift inside it. Something tall. Something watching.

She blinked, and it was gone.

Eddie whispered, "You saw it too, didn't you?"

She swallowed. "I saw nothing."

CENTRAL CITY

THE FOOD TRUCK PLAZA

The fog thickened as Caroline and Uncle Eddie made their way through the food-truck plaza, weaving between clusters of fans in Staffies and Mastiffs jerseys. Stadium lights glowed like blurred halos overhead, their beams swallowed by the winter haze rolling in.

“Man, it’s getting chilly out here,” Caroline muttered, pulling her scarf tighter.

Uncle Eddie sniffed the air like a bloodhound. “This isn’t normal fog.”

She groaned. “Please don’t start.”

“I’m not starting,” he said, eyes narrowing. “I’m observing.”

“Same thing.”

They reached *Galactic Bytes*, the sci-fi-themed food truck glowing neon blue in the mist. A holographic alien wearing a chef’s hat flickered above the ordering window.

“Two Molten Tacos,” Caroline said, tapping her card. “Extra lava sauce.”

“You’re going to regret that,” Uncle Eddie warned.

“I regret most things,” she replied. “Might as well enjoy dinner.”

They found a small standing table near the edge of the plaza. The fog curled around their ankles like a living thing. Caroline took a bite of her taco and nearly moaned.

“Okay… these are out of this world.”

Uncle Eddie pointed at her with a tortilla chip. “They might literally be just that.”

She laughed. “Uncle Eddie, it’s a taco, not a UFO.”

He didn’t laugh back. Instead, he nodded toward the far end of the plaza, where a white medical trailer sat parked near the stadium’s north gate. A banner hung from the side:

VALLEY REGIONAL BLOOD SERVICES —

COMMUNITY DRIVE

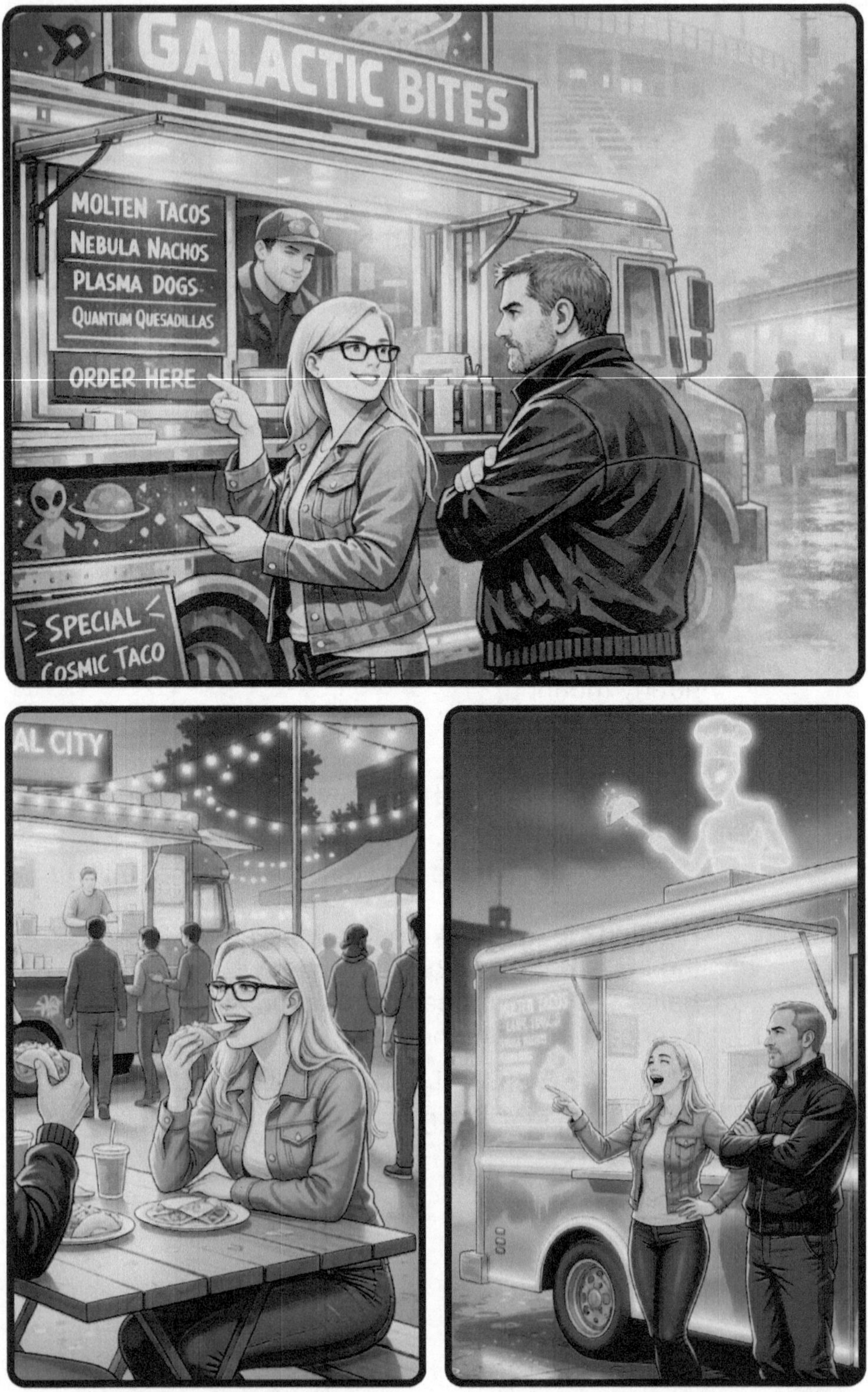

GALACTIC BITES
MOLTEN TACOS
NEBULA NACHOS
PLASMA DOGS
QUANTUM QUESADILLAS
ORDER HERE
SPECIAL
COSMIC TACO

AL CITY

The line seemed to have no end. A small army of nurses stood outside while student volunteers waved clipboards. The windows were tinted darker than regulation, and the generator hummed too quietly, like it was holding its breath.

“You see that?” Uncle Eddie asked.

“It's a blood drive.”

“It's a *collection point*,” he corrected. “A mobile feeding station. Look at all those people lined up to give blood. Are they sending out subliminal messages or something?”

Caroline rolled her eyes. “Oh boy. Here we go.”

“I'm serious,” he said. “Look at the fog around it. It's thicker there. Like it's being pulled in.”

“Fog doesn't get pulled in.”

“This fog does.”

She took another bite of her taco. “You're an old-school conspiracy theorist, you know that?”

“And you're a journalist who ignores the obvious.”

She smirked. “I'm a weather girl, remember?”

“You're more than that,” he said quietly. “You always have been.”

Something in his tone made her pause, but before she could respond, her phone buzzed.

PRODUCER:

Caroline,we need you in the press box for the halftime segment. Five minutes.

She sighed. “Duty calls.”

Uncle Eddie waved her off. “Go. I’ll… look around.”

“Promise me you won’t get arrested.”

“No promises.”

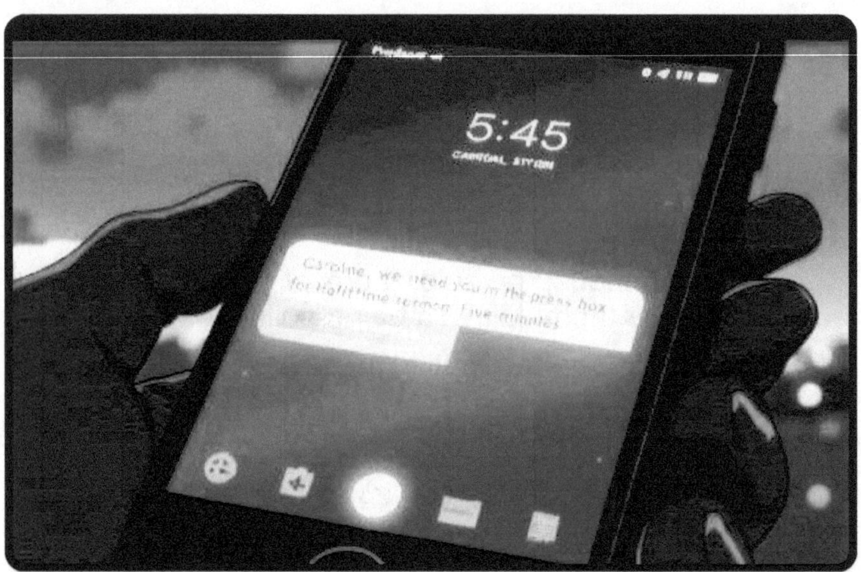

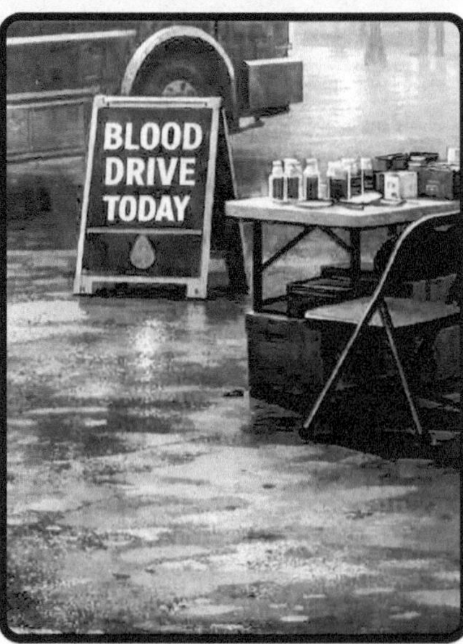

SECTION 112

Caroline cut through the back stairwell on her way to the press box, craving a moment of quiet before the halftime chaos. The fog had seeped into the concrete stairwell somehow, thin but present, curling along the edges like it was testing the boundaries.

Stopping beneath the hanging sign that read Section 112, she pulled a cigarette from her pocket, cupped her hand around it, and flicked her lighter.

Nothing. She flicked again. Still nothing.

“Seriously?” she muttered.

Footsteps echoed below. A maintenance worker rounded the corner, toolbox in hand, reflective vest half-zipped. He looked up, startled but polite.

“Hey,” Caroline said, lifting the useless lighter. “You got a light?”

He blinked, then smiled sheepishly. “Uh—yeah, actually.” He set his toolbox down and fished a shiny, polished brass lighter from his pocket. “These things never die.”

SECTION 112

She leaned in as he lit the end of her cigarette. "Thanks… Luis," she said, reading his name tag.

He nodded and gestured toward the stairwell door.

"On my way to check a breaker. One of the main stadium lights keeps tripping. Probably nothing, but they want it fixed before halftime."

"Sounds important."

He shrugged. "Everything's important on game night."

Caroline took a drag, exhaling into the fog. "Be careful down there. It's creepy as hell tonight."

Luis chuckled. "Tell me about it. Fog's been acting weird all week. Keeps setting off the motion sensors."

She raised an eyebrow. "Fog sets off sensors?"

"Yeah." He hesitated. "Moves like… I don't know. Like it's got weight."

A chill crawled up her spine.

"Well," she said, forcing a smile, "good luck with the breaker."

"Yeah. You too—with the weather report and all."

He picked up his toolbox. "Have a good night, Ms. MacGyver."

She blinked. "You know who I am?"

"Of course, you're on TV," he said with a grin. "Ms. MacGyver, can I ask you something?"

"Sure."

“Was your father really a spy?” he asked in a whispered tone.

It took every bit of mental energy she had not to lose her cool. With flared nostrils, she responded with a not-so-polite, “I don’t know what he did with his life, but whatever it was, it was more important than spending it here with my mother and me.”

“Okay… nice meeting you in person,” he said, and walked off into the stairwell.

They parted ways—Caroline heading up toward the stadium lights and noise, Luis descending into the dim corridor beneath Section 112. The roar of the crowd and the sounds of the bands swallowed everything.

THE PRESS BOX

Caroline reached the announcer's booth just as the Staffies scored a touchdown. The stadium erupted, shaking the glass. She set up her mic, adjusted her notes, and glanced out the window. That's when she saw it.

Across the field, in the far parking lot near the maintenance access road, a black SUV sat idling. Windows tinted. Headlights off. Engine running. Something about it tugged at her memory. She'd seen that SUV before, but where? A crime scene? A government building? She couldn't place it, but the unease settled in her stomach like a stone.

She snapped a picture with her phone, just in case.

As the announcer recapped the plays, Caroline found herself staring past him, studying the suspicious vehicle lurking in the fog. Then the commercials for the radio broadcast started.

“Brought to you by Central City Project Management—Always Moving Forward!”

Of course. CCPM. Those guys were always in the standard bad-guy jet-black SUV.

UNCLE EDDIE’S DETOUR

While Caroline called plays and read random trivia facts to the crowd, Uncle Eddie drifted toward the mobile blood bank. The fog was unnaturally thick around it, swirling in slow, deliberate patterns. He approached cautiously.

A figure in a white lab coat stepped out of the trailer, but something was wrong. The figure’s reflection in the trailer window lagged behind—a half-second delay, like a glitch in reality. Uncle Eddie’s breath caught.

The figure turned toward him.

“Can I help you?” the voice asked—too smooth, too calm.

Eddie opened his mouth to respond, but a security guard appeared out of nowhere.

“Sir, is there a problem?”

Eddie backed away slowly. “No problem. Just… curious.”

The guard didn’t blink. “Move along.”

Eddie did, but he didn’t stop watching.

CENTRAL CITY
MOBILE BLOOD BANK
GIVE BLOOD • SAVE LIVES
BLOOD
DRIVE
TODAY

HALFTIME

By halftime, the fog had swallowed half the field. Players vanished into it like ghosts. The announcers joked about"classic Central City weather," but **Caroline** felt a chill crawl up her spine.

As the high school marching bands played, she texted her uncle:

CAROLINE:

There is something fishy going on at the back end of the stadium. Where are you?

UNCLE EDDIE:

Following a lead.

She sighed. Of course he was.

All week she had been prepping for this game, making

sure she knew how to pronounce the players names correctly, what the different signals were that the ref used. She even reviewed some of the older games to get an idea on how she should sound. But now all she could think of was, *Who's in that SUV? and What are they upto?*

THE DISCOVERY

After the final whistle, fans poured out onto the field. The stadium became a chaotic river of cheers and trash talk. **Caroline** packed up her gear and headed toward the exit.

That's when she saw the flashing lights.

Police cruisers. Paramedics. Security guards blocking off the entrance to Section 112. A stretcher rolled out. Covered. Completely covered.

Caroline's breath hitched. "What happened?"

A security supervisor muttered, "Maintenance Tech working alone, looks like an accident. No foul play suspected."

She frowned. "Then why the police?"

"Ma'am, please step back."

Uncle Eddie appeared beside her, pale and shaken.

"Uncle Eddie... what did you see?" "I was over there at

the blood drive." He swallowed hard, eyes fixed on the fog-shrouded trailer. "Something's wrong."

"Did you see who was in the black SUV?"

"Wait, what? You saw a black SUV? Did you happen to get the plate number?" His concern sharpened instantly.

Chapter II — The Fog Keeps Secrets

The morning after the game, Central City woke to a blanket of fog so thick it muted the sunrise. The streets looked washed out and colorless, as if the world had been drained overnight.

Caroline sat at her kitchen table, coffee in hand, replaying the night in her mind. The covered stretcher, the police blocking off Section 112, the black SUV, and Eddie's pale face all looped through her thoughts.

She couldn't shake any of it.

Her phone buzzed.

WOLF 26 PRODUCER:
"Need you to follow up on the stadium incident. Police say 'medical emergency.' See what you can get."

Caroline snorted. "Yeah, because they're always so honest."

She grabbed her keys. If the police weren't talking, she'd find someone who would.

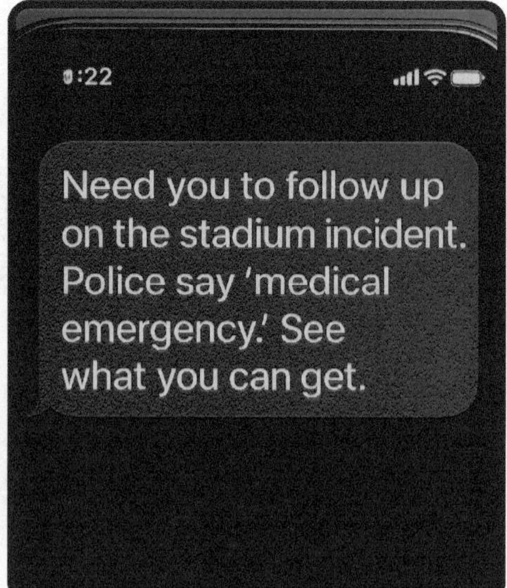

THE VICTIM

The stadium was closed to the public, but **Caroline** had a press badge and a smile that opened most doors.

She found a janitor sweeping the concourse, a man in his sixties with tired eyes.

"Excuse me," she said gently. "I'm with Wolf 26. I'm trying to confirm what happened last night."

He hesitated, looked around, then lowered his voice.

"Supervisor told us not to talk."

"Which means you should," she whispered. He swallowed. "His name was Luis. Maintenance. Good guy. Quiet. He was working under Section 112."

"Was?"

The janitor's broom slowed. "They found him… drained."

Caroline's heart skipped. "Drained how?"

He shook his head. "I didn't see. But the cops came fast. Too fast. Like they were waiting."

A chill crawled up her spine.

"Thank you," she said softly.

As she walked away, she texted Eddie.

CAROLINE:
We need to talk. This keeps getting weirder and weirder.

EDDIE'S DISCOVERY

Eddie lived in a unique building that he owned — a duplex apartment above a pawn shop. He occupied one unit and rented the other to a young guy, a skater-type who worked as a paramedic and kept odd hours. Eddie didn't care to know much about his tenant-slash-neighbor; the kid was quiet and paid rent on time, and that was enough for him.

As for Eddie's place, the front living room and dining area were immaculate. But behind the door that opened to the rest of the apartment, the walls were covered in

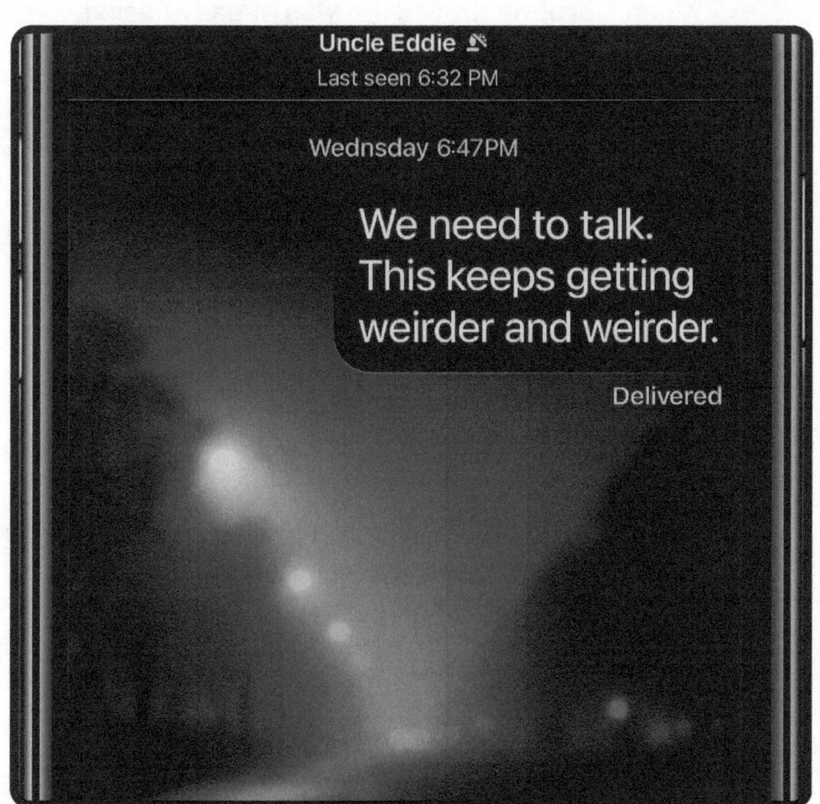
Uncle Eddie
Last seen 6:32 PM
Wednsday 6:47PM
We need to talk.
This keeps getting
weirder and weirder.
Delivered

EDDIE'S EXCHANGE
PAWN SHOP

maps, newspaper clippings, and red string — a conspiracy theorist's cathedral.

When **Caroline** arrived, he was already pacing.

"You heard about the victim?" she asked.

"I heard enough," Eddie said. "And I found something."

He motioned her over to his desk. A printed photo lay there — grainy, zoomed in, but unmistakable. The mobile blood bank. Except now, in the daylight, the trailer's side door was open. Inside were industrial refrigeration units.

Not medical-grade.

Not legal.

And the containers inside weren't labeled with blood types. They were labeled with **dates**.

On the back was a handwritten message:

Redwood Bay, CA. 01/01/2020.

Caroline felt her stomach twist. "What is this?"

"A harvesting station," Eddie said. "Not for donations. For storage."

"Storage of what?"

He met her eyes. "You know what."

She didn't want to say it. Not yet.

Instead, she asked, "Where did you get this photo?"

Eddie hesitated. "Someone sent it anonymously."

"Who?"

"I don't know."

But he did know. She could see it in his face. He just wasn't ready to say.

THE BLACK SUV RETURNS

Caroline decided to go back and do some more digging. The fog was thicker now, swirling in unnatural patterns and curling around streetlights like fingers.

As she turned onto Staffy Lane — the small service street behind the stadium — Caroline froze.

There.

Parked across the street, half-hidden in the fog, was the black SUV. Engine running. Headlights off. Same spot as last night.

She thought, *It's watching the stadium.*

Then she said aloud, "No… it's watching me."

The driver's window rolled down an inch — just enough for a small cloud of smoke to escape.

Caroline's pulse hammered. *I should go,* she thought, but she didn't move.

"That's not a cop," she murmured. "That's not a fan. That's someone who knows exactly what happened last night."

The SUV pulled away silently, disappearing into the fog like a ghost.

She walked the perimeter of the stadium, hoping to find where Luis had been found. The fog clung to the ground.

in thick, swirling patches. Then it shifted — not with the wind, not randomly. It moved around her, like it was aware.

Caroline stopped. “Fog doesn’t do that. Wait… but Uncle Eddie’s does,” she muttered.

A cold breeze swept past her, carrying a faint metallic scent.

Blood.

Caroline shivered.

She slipped through a maintenance door. She had picked up the art of lock-picking years ago during a “research expedition” with Uncle Eddie. She’d always been a fast learner — one lesson was all she ever needed for anything, and she could do it like a pro.

The corridor beneath Section 112 was dim, the lights flickering.

Caroline’s breath caught.

A smear of something dark stained the concrete floor. Not a pool. Not splatter.

A **drag mark**.

Leading toward a locked utility room.

As she knelt beside it, she thought, *This is a lot of blood for an accident. This looks bad.*

Caroline swallowed hard. “But just how bad…?”

He was drained.

The witness’s words hit her like a brick.

Then a voice echoed down the corridor.

"You shouldn't be here."

She spun around.

A large man stepped out of the shadows, dressed in a black turtleneck sweater. His presence filled the hallway like a threat. Square jaw. Cold eyes. A face nearly every Central City resident knew.
Ricardo Martino — "Pico the Guy."

Director of Security for Central City Project Management. One of the most feared men in the city. A man even some police answered to. She knew his younger cousins from high school — but that was years ago, when she was a kid.

He was much scarier now.

Caroline's throat tightened. "Mr. Martino… I was just—"

"Investigating," he finished. "I know. I hear you've become quite the detective lately."
"Yeah, well, not by choice. Weird things just keep happening around me." She stiffened. "You were at the game last night."

Pico didn't deny it. He stepped closer, lowering his voice.
"There was an incident. I tried to stop it. I failed."

Caroline's heart pounded. "Stop what?"

Pico's eyes flicked to the drag mark. "A death."

The word hung in the air like a blade.

Caroline could tell Pico was holding back. *Why say "a death" and not "a murder"?* she wondered.

He continued, voice low and controlled.

“There was an attack involving a maintenance worker. I intervened. And now the city is covering it up.”

“Why?” Caroline asked.

“Because panic is bad for business.”

He stepped back into the shadows.

“You didn’t see me. You didn’t hear this. And you’re going to stop digging.”

Caroline lifted her chin. “I can’t do that.”

Pico’s eyes narrowed. “I know.”

And then he was gone — swallowed by the fog.

Caroline leaned against the wall, breath shaking. “What did I just walk into?”

She stared down the dark corridor.

Deep in her gut, she knew.

Somewhere in the fog, something ancient was moving.

Something hungry.
And Central City had no idea.

Chapter III — The Cover Up

The fog didn't lift the next morning. If anything, it thickened—a heavy, suffocating blanket that swallowed the city block by block. Caroline drove slowly, headlights cutting only a few feet ahead, her mind replaying the night at the stadium. Luis Ortega, the drag marks, the blood bank, the black SUV, and Pico Martino's warning all churned in her thoughts.

She parked outside Wolf 26 News but didn't get out.

Her phone buzzed.

PRODUCER:

"Police released a statement. Stadium incident ruled accidental. No further comment."

Accidental. Right.

She stepped out of the car and nearly collided with a uniformed officer standing on the sidewalk.

“Ms. MacGyver?” he asked. Her stomach tightened.

“Yes?” He handed her a folded notice. “You’re requested
at Central City PD for a brief interview regarding last night’s incident.”

“Requested or required?”

He didn’t blink. “Strongly encouraged.”

She watched him walk away, disappearing into the fog like he’d never been there.

“Uncle Eddie is going to love this,” she muttered.

She got approval from her boss to go ahead and go right away, and to get whatever info she could on the accident from last night. Including any official statements from the detectives on the case.

CENTRAL CITY POLICE DEPARTMENT

The station lobby was quiet, clean, and empty. Too empty. A receptionist waved her through without checking ID or having her sign anything.

A detective waited in a small interview room,

Detective Ramos. She recognized him. One of Central City’s “Finest”. He was more than likely to be one of Pico’s men. Not officially, of course, but everyone knows who really has the power in Central City.

“Ms. MacGyver,” Ramos said, smiling without warmth. “Thanks for coming in.”

CENTRAL CITY
POLICE DEPARTMENT

She sat. “I didn’t have much of a choice.”

He ignored that. “We understand you were present at Staffordshire Stadium last night.”

“I was covering the game.”

“And you saw… what exactly?”

Caroline kept her voice steady. “A stretcher. Police. A blocked-off section. And a whole lot of fog.”

Ramos leaned forward. “Did you see the victim?”

“No.”

“Did you see anything unusual?”

She hesitated. The black SUV, the blood bank, the fog that moved like it was alive—all of it flashed through her mind.

“No,” she said. “Just the usual chaos of a rivalry game.”

Ramos studied her. “Good. Because the official ruling is accidental death. No foul play. No story.”

Caroline’s jaw tightened. “I decide what’s a story.”

“Not this time,” Ramos said. “Drop it.”

She stood. “Are we done?”

He nodded. “For now.”

As she walked out, she heard him speak quietly into his radio.

“She’s not backing off.”

Her pulse spiked. They were watching her.

BACK AT UNCLE EDDIE'S

Eddie opened the door before she knocked.

"I saw the fog," he said. "It's thicker today. It's reacting."

"To what?"

"To last night."

She stepped inside. "The police pulled me in. They told me to drop it."

Eddie snorted. "Which means you shouldn't."

She paced the room. "Uncle Eddie… first there's a murder, then Pico Martino shows up at the scene, now the police are actively trying to shut down any investigation?!"

Eddie froze. "Pico? Pico the Guy?"

"Yes."

Eddie rubbed his face. "Pico doesn't show up unless something really bad is about to happen."

Caroline stopped pacing. "Uncle Eddie… who is he really?"

Eddie hesitated. "He's… complicated."

"That's not an answer."

He sighed. "His father is one of the founding fathers of this city. My grandfather told stories about serving in the army during the time the Battle of Los Fresnos took place here in the valley back in the late 1800s. His family has been fighting vampires since before Central City existed. They're New Bloods—they age slow, heal fast, and they know things the rest of us don't."

Caroline stared at him. "His father was alive in the 1800s? That's like 200 years."

"He's old. Older than he looks. But not 200 years. Pico—born Emellio Ricardo Martino—was born in 1953."

"So he's… what? A vampire hunter?" she said, still in disbelief.

"Something like that." Eddie paused to sip his glass of rum and Coke. "And he's bound by secrecy."

"That, I can believe. He seemed like a guy who had a lot of secrets," she replied, pouring herself a glass of Eddie's cheap rum. She sank onto the couch. "So he sent you that photo?"

Eddie didn't deny it. "He can't expose the truth. But he can nudge people who aren't bound by contracts."

"People like us."

"People like you," Eddie corrected. "You're on TV."

"But Uncle Eddie, you have your own show on the radio dedicated to stuff like this."

"I'm a crazy old man with a microphone. Half of my audience listens to mock me, and the other half believes in stuff that even I would mock."

Caroline swallowed hard. "Uncle Eddie… what if we're in over our heads?"

He sat beside her. "We are. But that's never stopped us before."

You Again?

That night, **Caroline** drove home through the fog. The streets were empty. The city felt hollow. She turned onto her block and slammed the brakes.

The black SUV was parked across from her house. Engine running. Headlights off. Same as before.

Her heart pounded. She reached for her phone. Before she could dial, the driver's window rolled down. A silhouette. Broad shoulders. Cold eyes.

Pico Martino, again.

He stepped out of the SUV, fog curling around him like it recognized him.

"**Caroline,**" he said quietly. "We need to talk."

She didn't move. "Soo, I didn't get the message the first time and now you're here to threaten me?"

"No," he said. "I'm here to warn you."

"Warn me about what?"

He looked past her, toward the fog-shrouded street. "They know you're looking."

"Who?"

"The ones who killed Luis."

Her breath caught. "The vampire?"

Pico's face softened, and he nodded once. "It's still here. And it's watching you."

Caroline's skin prickled. "Why me?"

"Because you saw too much. And because you're not afraid."

She swallowed. "Should I be?"

"Yes," Pico said. "But don't stop."

She pulled the picture from her coat pocket and handed it to him. "Did you send this to my uncle?"

He examined the picture with a curious expression, looked at the back, and paused. His face shifted into something unreadable for just a split second.

"Doesn't matter who sent it," he said. "As long as it can lead you to the truth."

"The truth about what?" she asked.

"About what's coming."

"What is coming?" she pressed.

Pico stepped closer, voice low. "The Vampire Nation is moving again. And Central City is their first target."

Caroline felt the world tilt. Pico looked her in the eyes.

“Whatever you do… don’t trust the police. Don’t trust the city. And don’t go anywhere alone.”

He stepped back into the fog.

“And Caroline?”

She froze. “Yes?”

“If you see red eyes in the fog… run.”

The SUV vanished into the night.

And Caroline realized she wasn’t just reporting a story.

She was standing in the middle of a war.

Chapter IV

Another Day at The Office

Caroline didn’t sleep.

Every time she closed her eyes, she saw the drag marks under Section 112, the blood bank, the fog curling around Pico like it recognized him, and the way he said *run* like he’d said it before—to someone who didn’t.

By morning, the fog was worse. It pressed against her windows like a living thing, thick and gray and pulsing with slow, deliberate movement. She stood at her kitchen sink, staring out at the street, coffee cooling in her hands.

Something was out there. Watching. Waiting.

SECTION
112

She felt it in her bones—a pressure behind her ribs, a prickling at the base of her skull. It wasn't fear. Not exactly. More like awareness. She shook it off and grabbed her keys.

She had work to do.

THE BLOOD BANK TRAIL

Wolf 26 News Station was buzzing with morning chatter, but the moment **Caroline** walked in, the room went quiet. People glanced at her, then away. She ignored them and headed straight for her desk.

She pulled up the permit number from the mobile blood bank.
Sequoia County, CA.

She tried the company name.

Common Ranch LLC.

She checked the refrigeration unit serial numbers.
Reported stolen — Redwood Bay, CA.

January 1st, 2020.

Her breath caught. The date on the back of the photo.

She clicked deeper into the Redwood Bay incident. A local newspaper article popped up—short, vague, and clearly censored.

> "Unusual fog event disrupts New Year's celebrations.
> Several residents reported missing pets.
> One missing persons report filed."

OLF 26 NEWS

Common Ranch LLC
Asset Tracking Database - Refrigeration Units
Inventory
Serial Lookup
Incident Reports
Recent Searches:
CRX-7741
Redwood Bay thefts
PolarTech registry
Notes:
Serial Number
Model
Status
Location Reported
CRX-7741
PolarTech 9000
Reported Stolen
Redwood Bay, CA

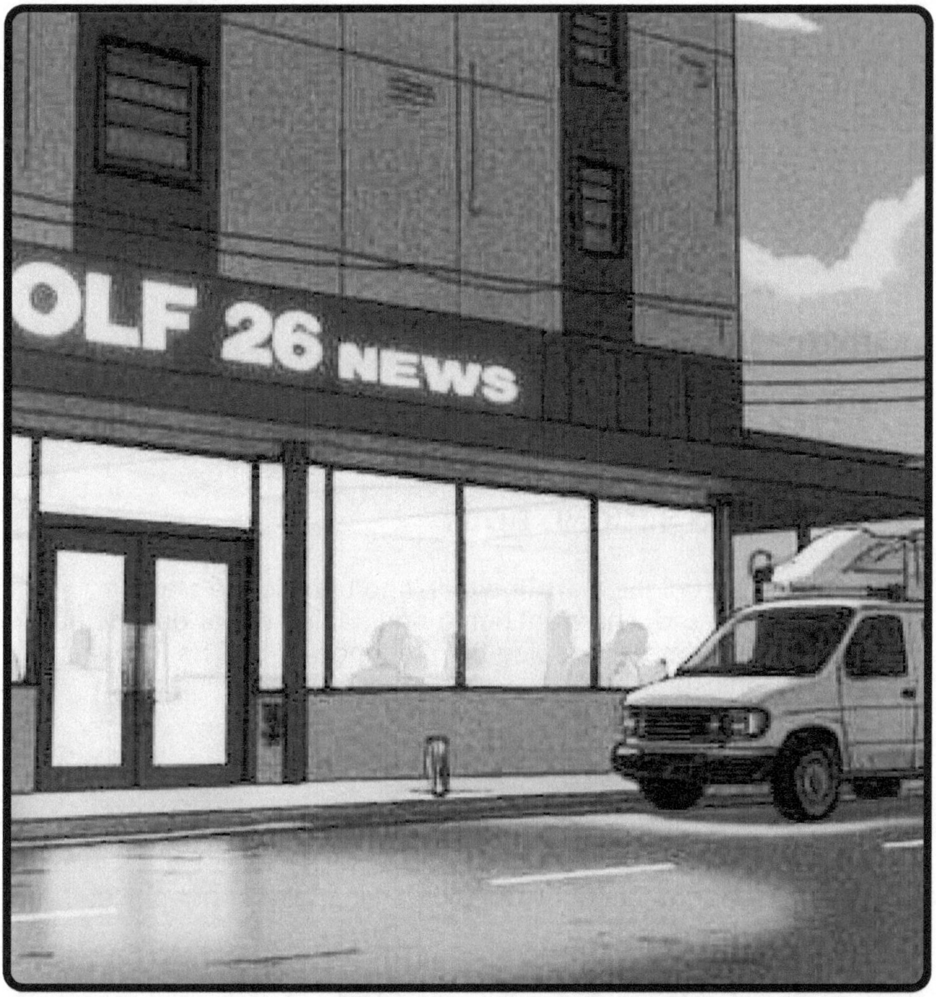

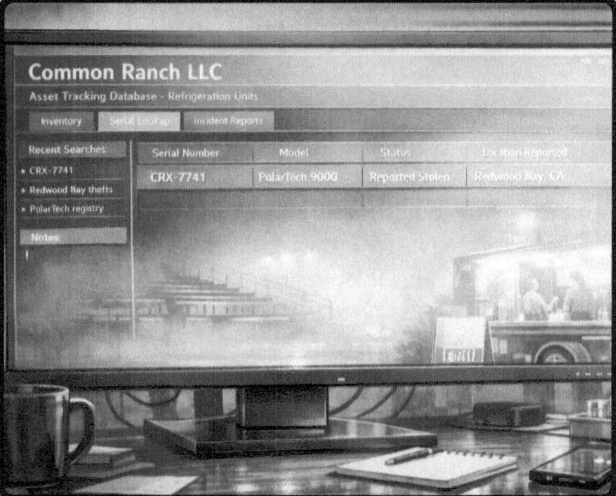

That was it. No follow-up. No investigation. No explanation.

She leaned back in her chair, heart pounding.

This wasn't a coincidence.

Someone wanted her to see this.

Someone who knew what the fog meant.
Someone who knew what was coming.

THE SECOND BODY

That night, **Caroline** didn't go back to the stadium. Instead, she went home and sat in her car outside her apartment, gripping the steering wheel. The fog was thicker than ever—a wall of gray swallowing the streetlights.

She stepped out into the cold air. The fog swirled around her ankles, curling like smoke, like fingers.
She walked down the narrow sidewalk along the row of apartments between the parking lot and her place.
And froze.

Her door was open—not wide, but just enough to see a glimmer of light through the crack.
Caroline's breath hitched. She approached slowly.

"Hello?" she called out, drawing her stun gun.

A shape lay slumped against the wall in her hallway. A man. Pale. Still. His eyes were open. His skin was gray. His lips were blue.

No blood. Not a drop.

Her stomach twisted. "Oh God…"

She knelt beside him, checking for a pulse she already knew wasn't there.

A faint metallic scent drifted through the fog.

Blood.

Something moved behind her. A whisper. A shift. A presence.

She spun around, but the fog swallowed everything.

Her heart hammered. "Uncle Eddie is going to freak out," she whispered.

She pulled out her phone to call 911—then stopped.

The police would cover this up.

Just like Luis.
Just like Pico said.

She took photos instead. Every angle. Every detail.

Then she backed away, pulse racing.

The fog followed her.

A cold breeze swept past her, carrying the metallic scent again.

Blood.

She shivered.

Something was coming.

Something old.
Something hungry.

But she felt it—deep in her bones.

She ran back to her car, grabbed the handle, and paused. Her hand trembled as she touched it.

The handle was cold. Too cold.

A whisper drifted through the fog behind her.

Not words.

A feeling.

Warning.

Her heart pounded. She backed away slowly.

The fog parted—just for a moment—revealing a tall, thin silhouette at the end of the street.

Not moving.

Not breathing.
Watching.

Red eyes flickered once.

Then vanished.

Caroline fumbled with her keys, got inside, and slammed the door.

Her pulse thundered.

Her instincts screamed.
Her bones ached.
Her senses sharpened.

Something inside her—something she didn't understand—was waking up.

She whispered into the cold air, "What the hell is going on?"

And somewhere in the fog outside was the answer.

WHO YOU GONNA CALL?

Caroline locked the doors, turned the ignition, and sat with her engine idling. Her breath came fast and shallow. The fog pressed against her windows like a living thing, pulsing with slow, deliberate movement.

She tapped the steering wheel nervously, stun gun still in her hand.

"Think, Caroline. Think."

The police were out.

Uncle Eddie would come running—but he'd get himself killed.

And the thing in the fog… it wasn't done.

Her phone buzzed in her pocket. She pulled it out. Her thumb hovered over 911.

She stopped.

Pico's voice echoed in her head:

> "Don't trust the police.
> Don't trust the city.
> And don't go anywhere alone."

Her pulse hammered. She scrolled to a number she never thought she'd use.

Pico Martino.

She hesitated only a second before pressing call.

The line rang once. Twice. Then:

"MacGyver."

He didn't say hello. He didn't sound surprised. He sounded like he'd been waiting.

Caroline swallowed hard. “Pico… something’s wrong.”

A pause. Not long—but long enough to tell her he already knew.

“What happened?”

“There’s a body,” she whispered. “In my apartment. A man. No blood. And the fog—it’s moving. It followed me. And something was watching me from the street.”

Another pause. Then Pico’s voice dropped, low and controlled.

“Are you inside?”

“No.”

“Are the doors locked?”

“Yes.”

“Good. Listen carefully.”

Caroline pressed the phone tighter to her ear.

“You’re not calling the police,” Pico said. “You’re calling me. That means you understand the situation better than you think.”

“I don’t understand anything,” she snapped, voice cracking. “There’s a dead man in my hallway, something with red eyes outside my door, and the fog is— it’s alive. I don’t know what’s happening.”

“You do,” Pico said. “You just don’t want to believe it.”

Her breath hitched. “Is it the same thing that killed Luis?”

“Probably,” Pico said.

Caroline's stomach twisted. "Why?" "You're the detective

here, not me. Can't you infer
context? Or whatever it is you guys do to solve your mysteries."

"I'm a journalist, not a detective—and technically I'm still just the weather girl."

"Only the weather girl, huh," Pico said, a long pause following. "Well, weather girl… whether you like it or not, someone seems to want you dead."

Her stomach churned. She squeezed the steering wheel harder.

"MacGyver," Pico said, voice steady, "you need to leave. Now."

"I can't just leave. There's a dead guy in there."

"I know," he said. "That's why you're not going back home tonight."

She blinked. "What?"

"You're going to a friend's house. A boyfriend. A relative. Anyone who can confirm you were with them all night."

"An alibi?" she whispered. "Why?"

"Because some people are going to go to your apartment to clean up this mess, and you can't be there when they do."

Her blood ran cold.

"And if you don't have an alibi," Pico continued, "the bad guys could try to make sure the evidence points to you."

Caroline's voice shook. "You're saying they'll frame me?"

"I'm saying," Pico replied, "that the people covering this up don't care who gets buried with the truth."

She pressed a hand to her forehead. "Okay. Okay. I can go to my uncle's place."

"Good. Leave now. Don't pack. Don't turn on any lights. Don't look back."

Caroline shifted her car into drive. "What about the thing in the fog?"

"It won't follow you," Pico said. "Not tonight."

"How do you know?"

A beat.

"Because it got what it came for."

Her breath caught. "The dead guy in my apartment?"

"Yes," Pico said quietly. "And if it wanted you, then you would be dead too."

Caroline froze. "What does that mean?"

But Pico didn't answer. Instead, he said:

"When you get to your uncle's, text me. And MacGyver—"

She swallowed. "Yeah?"

"Whatever you do… don't open the door for anyone. Not even if they sound like someone you know."

The line went dead.

SAFEHOUSE

Eddie's apartment sat above a pawn shop that hadn't changed its neon sign since the late '80s. The fog swallowed the street below, thick enough to muffle the hum of traffic. **Caroline** climbed the narrow staircase two steps at a time, her pulse still hammering from the drive over.

She knocked once.

The door swung open immediately.

Eddie stood there in pajama pants, a faded *Area 51 Fun Run* T-shirt, and a look that said he'd been pacing for the last hour.

"**Caroline?**" His voice cracked. "What happened? You okay?"

She didn't answer. She just stepped inside and locked the door behind her.

Eddie stared at her face, reading every tremor, every breath. "Sit. Talk. Now."

She dropped onto his couch—the same sagging brown monstrosity he'd had since she was twelve—and buried her face in her hands.

"There was a body in my apartment," she whispered. "A man. No blood. And the fog—it followed me, Uncle Eddie. It moved."

EDDIE'S EXCHANGE
PAWN SHOP

Eddie froze mid-step. “Moved how?”

“Like it was… aware.”

Eddie sat down slowly, like his knees had forgotten how to work. “And you called the police?”

She shook her head. “No.”

“Good,” he muttered. “Good girl.”

“I called Pico.”

Eddie’s head snapped toward her. “You what?”

“I didn’t know what else to do!”

He rubbed his face with both hands. “Oh, kiddo… that man is a walking classified file. You don’t call him unless you want your life to get complicated.”

“It’s already complicated,” she snapped. “He told me to come here. Said I needed an alibi.”

Eddie blinked. “An alibi?”

“Yeah. Because someone’s going to ‘clean up the mess’ at my place and I can’t be there when they do.”

Eddie let out a long, low whistle. “Well… that tracks.”

Caroline stared at him. “Uncle Eddie… what is happening to me?”

He didn’t answer right away. He stood, walked to the kitchen, poured a shot of cheap rum, and drank. Then said to himself, “Okay, time for the good stuff.” He reached into the cabinet over the fridge and pulled out a bottle of spiced rum—the imported stuff. He poured them both a drink and handed one to her.

She took it with shaking hands.

Eddie sat across from her, elbows on his knees. “Okay,” he said. “I need you to listen to me, and I need you not to freak out.”

“Uncle Eddie, I found a corpse in my hallway and something with red eyes was staring at me through the fog. I’m way past freaking out.”

He nodded. “Fair.”

He took a breath. “You’re… different, Caroline.”

She frowned. “Different how?”

“You’ve always been quick. Too quick. You pick things up after one lesson. You sense things before they happen. You don’t get sick. You don’t break bones. You don’t panic when you should. Just like…” He hesitated—not for drama, but because he knew how raw the topic was. “Just like your father was.”

“That’s not—that’s just me. I’m just lucky.”

“No,” Eddie said softly. “That’s New Blood.”

Caroline stared at him, the words hitting her like a physical blow.

“No,” she whispered. “No, Uncle Eddie, that’s—that’s Pico’s thing. His family’s thing. Not mine.”

Eddie shook his head. “It’s not just his family. It’s a gene. A rare one. And it runs in more than one bloodline.”

She swallowed hard. “You think I’m… like him?”

“I think,” Eddie said gently, “whatever is in the fog didn’t kill you tonight because it recognized you.”

Her breath caught. “What does that even mean?”

"It means..." Eddie paused. "Well, I think it means that whatever's out there... it doesn't see you as prey."

Caroline's skin prickled.

A sudden knock rattled the door.

Both of them froze.

Eddie mouthed: **Don't move.**

The knock came again, softer this time. Almost polite.

"**Caroline?**" a voice called. "It's Detective Ramos. We need to ask you a few questions."

Caroline's blood turned to ice.

Eddie leaned close, whispering into her ear. "Remember what Pico said. Don't open the door. Not even if they sound like someone you know."

The knock came again.

"Caroline," Ramos said, voice smooth, calm, practiced. "We know you're in there. We just want to talk."

Eddie mouthed: **He shouldn't know you're here.**

"My car is parked out front."

Caroline's heart pounded so hard she thought the detective might hear it through the door. The fog pressed against the windows. The lights flickered.

And somewhere outside, something moved.

Something that wasn't human.

Chapter V The Vampire's Message

Detective Ramos knocked again.

"Caroline," he called through the door, voice smooth as oil. "We just want to talk. Open up."

Eddie mouthed: **Don't move.**

Caroline held her breath. The fog outside pressed against the windows, dimming the streetlights until the room felt submerged underwater.

Ramos knocked a third time.

"Caroline… we know you're in there."

Eddie leaned close, whispering, "He shouldn't know that. He shouldn't know anything."

Caroline's pulse hammered. Her bones ached—a deep, instinctive warning she didn't understand.

Then, a sound.

Soft. Barely audible.

Like a breath being drawn in.

The fog outside shifted.

Not toward the door.
Away from it.

Ramos's voice faltered. "Caroline…?"

Silence.

Then footsteps retreating down the hall.

Eddie exhaled shakily. "He's gone."

"No," Caroline whispered. "Something scared him off."

Eddie's eyes widened. "Kid… what did you bring with you?"

Before she could answer, the lights flickered.

Once.

Twice.

Then, went out completely.

The room plunged into darkness.

Caroline's breath caught. "Uncle Eddie—"

"Stay behind me," he whispered, fumbling for a flashlight.

But the darkness wasn't empty.

Something moved in it.

A shape.
A presence.
A coldness that wasn't the fog.

Caroline felt it before she saw it—a pressure behind her ribs, a tightening in her throat, a strange clarity sharpening her senses.

Then a voice drifted through the dark.

Not human.
Not hostile.
Just… tired.

"You're not safe here. They're on to you."

Caroline froze. "Who's there?"

The flashlight clicked on.

A figure stood in the corner of the room—tall, thin, pale as moonlight. His clothes were torn, stained with dirt and fog. His eyes glowed faintly, not red, but a muted amber.

Eddie stumbled back. "Oh hell—"

The figure raised a hand. "Please," he said softly. "I'm not here to harm you."

Caroline's heart pounded. "You're the one from the stadium."

"Yes."

"You killed Luis."

"I did what was necessary."

His voice cracked—not with guilt, but with something like grief.

"He attacked me. I defended myself. He was a familiar. A slave. He was sent to silence me."

Caroline swallowed hard. "Silence you from what?"

The vampire stepped forward, slow and deliberate, hands open. "From telling the truth."

Eddie grabbed a silver letter opener from the table. "Stay back."

The vampire didn't flinch. "If I wanted you dead, you would be."

Caroline's skin prickled. He was right. She lowered her stun gun.

"What truth?"

The vampire turned to her—and for the first time, she saw fear in his eyes.

"My clan," he whispered. "They're planning a takeover. A political one. Central City is the first target."

Caroline's breath hitched. "Why tell me?"

"Because I tried to tell him."

"Pico?"

The vampire nodded. "He was the only human I trusted. The only one who might listen. But the familiars found me first. They followed me to the stadium. They tried to stop me."

Caroline's mind raced. "So the blood bank—"

“A harvesting station,” the vampire said. “Not for feeding. For control. Blood is power. Influence. Leverage. They’re building a network.”

Eddie whispered, “A political coup…”

“Yes.”

Caroline shook her head. “Why me? Why now?”

The vampire stepped closer, voice low. “Because the one leading the takeover knows who you are. And he fears what you might become.”

Caroline’s heart pounded. “Who is he?”

The vampire hesitated. Then whispered a name.

“**Kaleth.** She is my Queen and ruler of the Vampire Nation. And I am **Vaelor**, a servant of the Queen’s court. I was one of her personal bodyguards.”

Eddie went pale.

Caroline felt the name echo through her bones.

Before she could speak, the vampire stepped back into the shadows.

“They’re coming,” he whispered. “And you must choose who you stand with.”

The fog outside surged against the windows.

The lights flickered back on.

Vaelor was gone.

Caroline stood frozen, heart racing, the name echoing in her skull.

Eddie didn't move for a long moment. He just stared at the spot where Vaelor had been standing, as if expecting the vampire to reappear and say he'd forgotten something. The fog outside pressed harder against the windows, swirling in slow, deliberate patterns that made **Caroline's** skin crawl.

Finally, Eddie dragged a hand down his face. "Okay. Okay. We need a plan."

Caroline let out a shaky breath. "A plan for what? A vampire queen? A political coup? Fog that moves like it's alive? Eddie, I'm barely keeping up."

"You're keeping up better than most humans would," he muttered. "Which is part of the problem."

She shot him a look. "Not helping."

He held up his hands. "Right. Sorry. Just… give me a second to process the fact that a royal vampire bodyguard just dropped into my living room to warn us about a supernatural coup."

Caroline paced the room, running her hands through her hair. "Vaelor said Kaleth knows who I am. How? Why? I'm nobody."

Eddie shook his head. "Kid, you're not nobody. Not to them."

"That's not comforting."

"It wasn't meant to be."

Caroline stopped pacing and stared at the fog-blurred window. "If Kaleth knows who I am… does Pico?"

Eddie hesitated. "I think Pico suspects. Maybe more than suspects."

She turned toward him. "And he didn't tell me?"

"He can't," Eddie said. "He's bound by secrecy. You know that."

"That didn't stop him from warning me."

"That was different. You were in danger."

"I'm still in danger."

Eddie opened his mouth, then closed it again. "Yeah. You are."

The room fell quiet. The only sound was the faint hum of Eddie's old refrigerator and the distant, muffled swirl of fog outside.

"We need to talk to Pico," Caroline said.

Eddie nearly choked. "Absolutely not."

"He knows more than he's saying."

"He always knows more than he's saying."

"He's the only one Vaelor trusted."

"Vaelor also said familiars tried to kill him. You want to be next?"

Caroline crossed her arms. "Pico is the only person in this city who understands what's happening. And he's the only one who might know how to stop it."

Eddie rubbed his temples. "Kid, you're walking into a storm."

"I'm already in it."

He sighed. "Fine. But we do this smart. We don't call him. We don't text him. We go and speak in person."

"Where?"

STAFFORDSHIRE
FARMS
EST. 1952
PolarTech 9000
Report
LOCALLY GROWN · FRESH PRODUCE

“There’s only one place Pico goes when he doesn’t want to be found.”

Caroline raised an eyebrow. “And you know this how?”

Eddie hesitated, then groaned. “Because I’ve been keeping tabs on Pico for years.”

“Why? Because he’s scary?”

“No. Because ten years ago I watched two of the Martino family pitbulls get sucked into the sky by a frikken UFO. I filmed the whole thing. Bright lights, humming noise, dogs levitating—the works.”

Caroline stared at him. “Uncle Eddie…”

“Don’t start. I know what I saw. And Pico was there that night. He showed up out of nowhere, shut down the whole ranch, and told me if I valued my sanity I’d forget everything. The next day Regina Martino shows up at the station and offers a ridiculous amount of money to buy out the radio station. She said I could keep running it like it was mine, just as long as I didn’t do any stories about them or the ranch. So I took it. I used the money to buy this pawn shop.”

“You took the money?”

“Hell yes. That was the moment I realized Pico wasn’t just some gangster. He was involved in something bigger. So yeah, I took the money—and I’ve been ‘monitoring’ him ever since.”

Caroline grabbed her jacket. “Then let’s go.”

“Not yet,” Eddie said. “We wait until the fog thins. And until we’re sure Ramos isn’t lurking outside.”

Caroline glanced at the door. “Do you think he’ll come back?”

"Not while Vaelor's scent is still in the air."

She shivered. "That's… comforting?"

"Not really."

They sat in uneasy silence, the weight of Vaelor's warning hanging between them.

Caroline finally whispered, "Eddie… what if Kaleth really is coming?"

Eddie looked at her with a seriousness she'd never seen before. "Kid… if Kaleth is coming, then Central City is already in trouble."

Caroline swallowed hard. "Then we'd better get ahead of it."

Eddie nodded. "Yeah. We'd better."

Outside, the fog shifted again— Like it was waiting.

Chapter VI — The Confrontation Begins

The fog thinned just enough for the streetlights to glow like dying embers. Eddie peeked through the blinds, scanning the parking lot twice before nodding.

“Alright. The coast looks clear. Grab your jacket.”

Caroline buttoned up her jacket, still feeling the phantom pressure of Vaelor’s presence lingering in her bones. “So we’re going to Staffordshire Farms?”

“That was the plan,” Eddie said, locking the door behind them. “But we’ll see how far we get.”

They hurried down the narrow staircase, the fog curling around their ankles like curious hands. Eddie’s beat-up Subaru sat crooked in its spot, headlights dimmed by the mist. Caroline slid into the passenger seat, her nerves buzzing like static.

Eddie started the engine. “We stick to the back roads. Less chance of running into Ramos or anyone else who shouldn’t be out tonight.”

They pulled out of the lot, the fog parting just enough to let the car pass. Caroline watched it in the side mirror—the way it shifted, the way it moved with intention.

"Eddie," she said quietly, "what if Vaelor was right? What if Kaleth really does know who I am?"

Eddie tightened his grip on the wheel. "Then we need answers. And the only person who might give them to us is Pico."

They drove in silence for several minutes, the city fading behind them as the outskirts of Central City stretched into orchards and farmland. The fog thinned, then thickened again, rolling across the fields like a living tide.

Caroline leaned forward. "Do you think Pico will actually talk to us?"

"He'll talk to you," Eddie said. "He always does."

Caroline frowned. "What's that supposed to—"

A pair of headlights appeared behind them.

Close.

Too close.

Eddie checked the mirror. "Damn it."

"What?"

"That's a police cruiser."

Caroline's stomach dropped. "Ramos?"

"Or someone working for him."

The cruiser followed them for a full minute, silent, steady, unblinking.

Then the sirens lit up.

Red and blue flashed across the fog.

"Eddie," Caroline whispered, "don't stop."

"I wasn't planning on it."

He pressed the accelerator. The Subaru lurched forward, tires kicking up gravel as they sped down the rural road. The cruiser followed instantly, sirens screaming through the night.

"They're gaining!" Caroline shouted.

"They're in a Crown Vic, kid—they're always gaining!"

The cruiser swerved, trying to bump their rear bumper. Eddie jerked the wheel, barely keeping them on the road.

"They're trying to run us off!" Caroline yelled.

"No kidding!"

The cruiser rammed them again, harder this time. The Subaru fishtailed, skidding dangerously close to the ditch.

"Eddie!" Caroline grabbed the dashboard. "We're not gonna make it!"

"Hold on!"

The cruiser lined up for another hit.

And then—

Headlights appeared out of the fog.

Black.

Silent.
Massive.

The SUV.

It roared out of the mist like a charging bull and slammed into the police cruiser from the side. Metal crunched. Glass exploded. The cruiser flipped twice, skidding into a ditch in a shower of sparks.

Eddie slammed on the brakes. The Subaru screeched to a stop sideways across the road.

Caroline's breath came in sharp, panicked bursts. "Oh my God… oh my God…"

Eddie stared at the wreck. "Kid… stay in the car."

Two figures crawled out of the overturned cruiser—Detective Ramos and his partner. Both were bleeding, dazed, but alive. They drew their guns and opened fire on the SUV.

The black vehicle's door swung open.

Pico stepped out.

He didn't flinch as bullets tore into the SUV's armored frame. He didn't shout. He didn't warn them. He simply raised his weapon—a compact, fully automatic, absolutely illegal pistol—and returned fire with cold precision. The gunfight erupted into chaos—muzzle flashes lighting the fog, bullets slicing through the night, the air thick with smoke and adrenaline.

Caroline watched in stunned disbelief. "Eddie… what is happening?"

"Something bad," Eddie whispered. "Something really bad."

Then the fog shifted. A shape emerged behind the detectives.

Tall. Thin. Silent.

Vaelor.

He moved faster than Caroline could track—a blur of pale motion. In seconds, the gunfight ended. The detectives collapsed, their weapons clattering to the ground.

Caroline's breath caught as Vaelor knelt beside one of them. She couldn't look away. She couldn't blink. She couldn't breathe.

Eddie whispered, horrified, "Kid… don't watch."

But she did.

Vaelor fed.

Not with gore or violence, but with a terrifying, unnatural efficiency. A predator reclaiming strength. A creature doing what it was made to do.

Caroline's heart pounded so hard she thought it might burst.

Pico lowered his weapon, staring at Vaelor with a mixture of fury and resignation.

Chapter VII — Terms of Survival

The gunfire faded into the fog, leaving only the ringing in **Caroline's** ears and the distant hiss of cooling metal. The overturned police cruiser smoked in the ditch, its headlights flickering weakly against the grass. Vaelor stood over the fallen detectives, his chest rising and falling with slow, controlled breaths as he wiped the corner of his mouth with the back of his hand.

Caroline couldn't move. Eddie couldn't speak. The world had narrowed to the impossible scene in front of them.

Then the SUV door slammed.

Pico stepped out.

He didn't look at the bodies. He didn't look at Vaelor. He walked straight toward Caroline and Eddie, his expression carved from stone.

"Out of the car," he said.

Eddie swallowed hard. "Pico—"

"Now."

They stepped out, the cold night air hitting them like a slap. Caroline's legs trembled, but she forced herself to stand tall. Pico stopped a few feet away, hands at his sides, eyes sharp and unreadable.

"You two nearly got yourselves killed," he said. "Again."

Caroline found her voice. "Those detectives tried to run us off the road!"

"Yes," Pico said. "Because they were the ones helping the Vampire Nation gain ground in Central City."

Eddie blinked. "Ramos? A mole?"

"Not just a mole," Pico said. "They were the pipeline. Every missing person, every unexplained fog event, every cover-up—they were the ones making sure it never reached daylight."

Caroline's stomach twisted. "And you knew?"

"I suspected," Pico said. "But I didn't know who. Not until you stumbled onto the case."

Caroline stared at him. "So you used me."

Pico didn't flinch. "Yes."

Eddie stepped forward. "You son of a—"

Pico raised a hand. "I didn't put you in danger. The moment you started digging, you were already in danger. I just… let the wrong people show their hand."

Caroline's voice cracked. "You used me as bait."

"I used you as a spotlight," Pico corrected. "And it worked."

Caroline shook her head. "You could have told me."

"No," Pico said. "If I told you, you would have acted differently. They would have noticed. And they would have probably gotten to you before I could intervene."

Caroline looked away, jaw tight. "I trusted you."

Pico's voice softened—barely. "And I trusted you to survive."

A silence settled between them, heavy and cold.

Then Vaelor stepped forward.

Pico turned to him, eyes narrowing. "You shouldn't have revealed yourself."

“I had no choice,” Vaelor said. His voice was calm, but there was a tremor beneath it. “Your hunters were closing in. And I am no longer welcome among my clan.”

Caroline stared at him. “You’re exiled?”

Vaelor nodded. “For acting against the Queen. For warning you. For refusing to take part in the coup.”

Eddie crossed his arms. “So what, you want asylum?”

Vaelor met Pico’s gaze. “I want protection. And in return, I will help you stop her.”

Pico studied him for a long moment. “You’re a liability.”

“I am also the only one who knows her next move,” Vaelor said. “And the only one who can get you close enough to stop it.”

Caroline stepped forward. “Why help us at all?”

Vaelor’s amber eyes softened. “Because Kaleth will not stop with Central City. She will not stop with humans. She will not stop with New Blood. She will not stop until every clan kneels or burns.”

Pico exhaled slowly. “So you’re defecting.”

“I am surviving,” Vaelor said. “And I am offering you the same chance.”

He turned to Caroline and Eddie.

“You two need to listen carefully,” Pico said. “Because after tonight, nothing about your lives stays the same.”

Caroline stiffened. “What does that mean?”

“It means,” Pico said, “you change everything. Your routines. Your routes. Your habits. Your friends. Your schedule. You don't walk alone at night. You don't go jogging in the park. You don't answer your door unless you know who's on the other side. You don't chase stories that smell like fog."

Caroline swallowed. "So I just… stop?"

"Yes," Pico said. "You stop. You drop this story. You go back to weather reports and human-interest fluff pieces. You pretend none of this ever happened."

Eddie stepped forward. "You can't expect her to just—"

"I can," Pico snapped. "Because Kaleth knows her name now. And she doesn't let loose ends walk around breathing."

Caroline's voice cracked. "So what am I supposed to do? Hide?"

"Survive," Pico said. "That's the job now."

He reached into the SUV and pulled out a small black case. He opened it and handed her a compact weapon—sleek, matte, unfamiliar.

Caroline stared at it. "What is this?"

"Insurance," Pico said. "It won't kill a vampire. But it'll make one think twice."

Eddie bristled. "You're arming her but telling her to quit? That's backwards."

Pico turned to him, eyes cold. "I'm giving her a chance to live. You want to argue philosophy, do it on your own time."

Eddie stepped closer. "You used her, Pico. You put her in the crosshairs."

"And I pulled her out," Pico said. "Don't forget that part."

Eddie clenched his jaw. “You don’t get to play hero.” “I’m not a hero,” Pico said. “I’m the one cleaning up the mess.”

Vaelor stepped forward, his voice low. “We should go. The Queen’s guards will sense the blood soon.”

Pico nodded. “Get in the SUV.”

Vaelor obeyed without hesitation.

Pico turned back to Caroline one last time. “You want the truth? Here it is. You were bait. And you were good at it. But now the game changes. You stay alive by staying out of the way.”

Caroline’s eyes burned. “And what about you?”

“I go where the war is,” Pico said. “And right now, it’s not with you.”

Eddie stepped protectively in front of her. “If you think I’m letting you drag her into this again—”

“You’re not letting me do anything,” Pico said. “You’re going home. Both of you. You’re going to pretend this night never happened.”

Caroline’s voice trembled. “Pico… what if she doesn’t?”

Pico paused—just long enough to show he’d considered that possibility.

“Then you’ll know,” he said quietly, “because the fog will come for you first.”

He climbed into the SUV. The engine rumbled to life.

Vaelor watched them through the tinted window, unreadable.

Eddie wrapped an arm around Caroline's shoulders as the black SUV disappeared into the fog.

For a long moment, neither of them spoke. The night was too quiet. The fog too still. The world too changed.

Finally, Caroline whispered, "…what do we do now?"

She stared at the empty road, the weapon heavy in her hand.

"We go home," Eddie said. "And we try to pretend we're normal."

She nodded slowly. "Think we can pull that off?"

Eddie didn't answer.

The fog curled around their feet like a warning.

She tightened her grip on the weapon. "Eddie," she whispered, "I don't think anything is ever going to be normal again."

They stood there together, two small figures in a vast, shifting night.

And somewhere far beyond the fog, something ancient stirred.

Caroline will Return…

Epilogue: The Handwriting

Caroline sat alone at the kitchen table, the photo between her fingers. The edges were worn now, curled from being handled too many times. She turned it over again.

The handwriting on the back — the message she'd thought came from Pico — was neat, deliberate. But suspicious.

She knew something was off. She'd seen enough murder mysteries to think that she could actually believe that Pico isn't hiding something about this still. She got on her Lap top and searched. She went though city contract records, archive files, any thing she could think of to find it. And finally she found it, on the weapon registration. Pico's signature. It Didn't match the handwriting on the back of the photo.

This wasn't his.

Her breath caught. The room felt colder.

Not Pico's.

She stared at the photo again. At the message.

Redwood Bay, CA. 01/01/2020.

Her fingers trembled.

Outside, the fog was rolling in again.

After the Fog Settled

A Note From the Creator

Stories like this don't come together alone. They're stitched from late-night ideas, quiet moments, and the tools that help turn imagination into something you can hold in your hands.

This book was shaped with the help of:

• Microsoft Copilot

For walking beside me through every twist in the road — brainstorming, refining, and helping me chase the story through the fog.

• ArtSpace AI

For giving form to the scenes that lived in my head — the roads, the mist, the shadows, the faces — and letting me *see* the world as it unfolded.

• Canva

For turning pages into something polished, cohesive, and worthy of the story they carry.

Together, these tools helped bring Caroline, Eddie, Pico, and Vaelor out of the dark and into the light — or at least into the fog.

And to you, the reader:

Thanks for walking this road with us.

www.ingramcontent.com/pod-product-compliance
Lightning Source LLC
LaVergne TN
LVHW090532110826
845146LV00003B/1073

* 9 7 9 8 9 9 3 4 4 4 9 2 5 *